The Roxy Hunter Files

Case #2:

The Secret of the Shaman

CONFIDENTIAL!

By Robin Dunne and James Kee

Based on the television movie screenplay by

Robin Dunne and James Kee

123 * Roxy Hunter Case Files *

0 0 5 0 **PRIVATE** 0 0

R

PSS!
PRICE STERN SLOAN

PRICE STERN SLOAN
Published by the Penguin Group
Penguin Group (USA) Inc., 375 Hudson Street, New York,
New York 10014, USA
Penguin Group (Canada), 90 Eglinton Avenue East, Suite 700,
Toronto, Ontario M4P 2Y3, Canada
(a division of Pearson Penguin Canada Inc.)
Penguin Books Ltd., 80 Strand, London WC2R 0RL, England
Penguin Group Ireland, 25 St. Stephen's Green, Dublin 2, Ireland
(a division of Penguin Books Ltd.)
Penguin Group (Australia), 250 Camberwell Road, Camberwell,
Victoria 3124, Australia (a division of Pearson Australia Group Pty. Ltd.)
Penguin Books India Pvt. Ltd., 11 Community Centre, Panchsheel Park,
New Delhi—110 017, India
Penguin Group (NZ), 67 Apollo Drive, Rosedale, North Shore 0632,
New Zealand (a division of Pearson New Zealand Ltd.)
Penguin Books (South Africa) (Pty.) Ltd., 24 Sturdee Avenue,
Rosebank, Johannesburg 2196, South Africa

Penguin Books Ltd., Registered Offices:
80 Strand, London WC2R 0RL, England

Library of Congress Control Number: 2007010517

ISBN 978-0-8431-2666-2   10 9 8 7 6 5 4 3 2 1

✲ GUESS WHAT?! ✲

The most amazing thing is happening tomorrow!
(No, I'm not getting a hot-air balloon.)
The spectacular, fantabulous* writer Mr. Lorne
Red Deer is reading to our day camp tomorrow!
He authorizes* my favorite series of books—
Tanaka the Orphan Warrior!

Hello. This is Max. I've
been asked to go through
Roxy's journal and try to
make clear her unique use
of words—or "mangulations,"
as she would call them.

Facts from the desk of: **MAX**

Roxy Word: *fantabulous:
Max Fact: fantastic + fabulous

Roxy Word: *authorizes:
Max Fact: authors/writes:
to write a book

As super sensational as the Tanaka books are,
I do feel they lack one essential ingredient:
This. My creation.

ISN'T SHE
AMAZING?!

This is Princess
Roxahana, a warrioress
and near-orphan.

A POEM
BY ROXY HUNTER
Who is this warrior
with such might?
It's Roxahana, for
good she'll fight.
Alone she wanders on the range
With adventures both weird and strange.
She runs with elk and buffalo
And roasts at night the marshmallow.

What a Great Day!

(Most of it.) I met the celerybated* Mr. Lorne Red Deer! He read to us from his brand-new book Tanaka and the Curse of the Caribou.

It was **<u>undebeleezado!</u>**

I rank Mr. Red Deer up there with Joyce James and Virginia Woof*. I talked to him after and he said he remembered my letters to him! I was very flattered. And he said he would read my Roxahana ideas! But first I had to have Mr. Red Deer sign a non-disposure* contract to protect my creation.

Facts from the desk of: **MAX**

Roxy Word: *celerybated:

Max Fact: celebrated

Roxy Word: *Joyce James & Virginia Woof:

Max Fact: James Joyce & Virginia Woolf—two famed authors

Roxy Word: *non-disposure contract:

Max Fact: nondisclosure contract: an agreement promising to keep a secret

NON-DISPOSURE CONTRACT

This is a legal document guaranteeing that I, Roxy Hunter, being of sound mind, am the sole creator of the character "Princess Roxahana, the warrioress and near-orphan" and own all rights of this character in perpetuosity* throughout the universe and beyond for all time forever. This document is legal and blinding*. Stamped it. No erasees.

Ugknowledged* and signed,

YOUR NAME HERE.

Facts from the desk of: **MAX**

Roxy Word: *perpetuosity:
Max Fact: perpetuity: forever

Roxy Word: *blinding:
Max Fact: binding

Roxy Word: *ugknowledged:
Max Fact: acknowledged

However, the day was not without its grimosity*.

This is MS. SLAUSEN.

Pardon me, "Sauerkraut" Slausen.

She is the head of day camp.

This is a place you get sent
to during summer holidays if
your parents are at work.
We do arts and crafts, and
it would be fun, except...

MS. SLAUSEN HATES ME. No. Really. She does.

My dear journal, you know I always try to think
the best of people.

I really do.
But she makes
it tough.
REALLY TOUGH.
She is my
nemanosis*.

Facts from the desk of: MAX

Roxy Word: *grimosity:

Max Fact: It probably means really
bad. This is a "Roxyism." She has
taken a word (like "grim") and created
her own word.

Roxy Word: *nemanosis:

Max Fact: nemesis:

an unbeatable enemy

The reason she gave me trouble was because I was trying to tell raisin-brain Seth and the double-dimwit-twins to stop talking while Mr. Red Deer was reading to us. And Slausen got mad at me for talking! **ME**—his biggest fan! The absurdosity* of the situation! Is there no justice, I ask you?!

Facts from the desk of: **MAX**

Roxy Word: *absurdosity:

Max Fact: absurdity: ridiculousness

By the way...

Seth was telling the story of a boy named ANDY who was walking through the Black Marsh Forest the other night, and just so happened upon...

A MONSTER!

The legend says that there have been strange noises and stuff coming from the marsh for years and years.

This demands a certificated*
ROXY HUNTER SUPERSLEUTH INVESTIGATION!

Facts from the desk of: **MAX**

Roxy Word: *certificated:
Max Fact: certified

9

the Black Marsh Monster
Artist's renderition*.

(Note—if I don't make it
back alive, I hereby donate
all my earrings to the
Serenity Falls Foundation
for Eaten Children.)

Facts from the desk of: **MAX**

Roxy Word: *renderition:

Max Fact: rendition: an interpretation

I am pleased to announce the arrival of my brand-new sidekick!

SWIFTFOOT!

Okay, okay—here's what happened. While I went to search for the marsh monster, I met a stray dog! He came right up to me! He is such a friendly and smart K-9, I think he could be a K-10! And he says he wants to be my sidekick. He told me so. I believe one bark means "yes" in dog language, and two means "yes, indeed!" Dogs don't often say no to anything.

(Come on, they even eat garbage.)

Roxy Word: *formularating:

Max Fact: formulating: to carefully create something

Why is a sidekick so important?

Ah! Glad you asked, oh journal.

Well, they are the ultimate accessory for any great detective sniffing out clues. They are simply a **"MUST-HAVE."**

The difficulty with sidekicks is sneaking them past Mom, when she has said that I can't have a dog. But a great detective always has a plan. And I am formularating* one.

So far it involves a *trampoline* and a *doggie cape*.

I will keep you updated.

So—I had to get my sidekick into the house; I had to investigate the BLACK MARSH MONSTER; and to top it off, Deputy Sheriff Potts came by and warned us that someone was stealing flags and decorations in town. (Mom and Jon are on the sesquicemteminal* decoration committee.) Apparently EVERY mystery in town weighs on my young shoulders!

Jon called Potts a nickname— "Bull." Apparently, a long time ago, Potts brought the school mascot to a dance. The mascot was a bull. The dance was for Valentine's Day. Think about it.

Bull + red Valentine's decorations = DISASTER!

And so ever since, they call him "Bull."

Facts from the desk of: **MAX**

Roxy Word: *sesquicemteminal:

Max Fact: sesquicentennial: 150th anniversary or birthday

Oh.

And how could I forget?
The wedding may be off.
This is Jill.
She has bent Max to
her will. Using her evil skill.
Max is tutoring Jill in French. The language of love.
*Nest paw?**

She called him "Maxie" and made
him blush. MADE HIM BLUSH*!

He is **MY FIANCÉ**.

If anyone is going to make him blush,
it's ME! THE NERVE! I can only hope Max
stays strong. Because I can tell that Jill is up
to something.

Facts from the desk of: **MAX**

Roxy Word: *Nest paw:*
Max Fact: n'est pas: French for
"isn't it?"
And I wasn't blushing.

Back to...

Feeding a homeless, hungry, hairy dog (soon to be sidekick!). A hungry dog is like a hungry child—but with four legs instead of two. I've got to get some food to him. But how? Wait! A plan formularates*! It's going to take some artful dodgering and some sneakification*, but that's how we sleuths roll.

MAY I PRESENT TO YOU, OH JOURNAL . . .

Facts from the desk of: **MAX**

Roxy Word: *formularates:

Max Fact: formula + accelerate = to form a plan quickly

Roxy Word: *dodgering & sneakification:

Max Fact: Roxyisms

OPERATION SWIFTFOOT

Hide food in laundry basket.

Slip past guards.

Put food in knapsack.

Put laundry under sheets
to look like a sleeping Roxy.

Slip out window and
save starving dog!

My plan worked! (Naturally.)

I met SWIFTFOOT in the field behind my house.
And he was waiting for me—just like I knew he would
be! He took some food, but then ran off into the
woods! *Sidekicks aren't supposed to do that.*
I decided to bring him up to date on the rules
of his new job. So I followed him.

Don't start with me, journal.

I know I'm not allowed to go into the forest at
night, but I am completely capable of handling myself
in the creepy, dark woods, *thankyouverymuch.*
Okay... So maybe next time I'll bring Max
along as backup.

And in the scary, spooky woods was where (IT) happened.

I heard a crackle.
I heard a krinkle.

And SOMETHING MOVED in the dark.

I realized it could only be one thing...

THE BLACK MARSH MONSTER!!

I started to run, but I slipped and fell!

I landed okay, but when I looked up...

But instead of eating me...
It asked if I was okay.
It wasn't a monster—it was
a man. And then Swiftfoot
came up and started licking

his hand. THEY WERE FRIENDS!
The man was so nice, and had kind but sort of
sad eyes. So when he and Swiftfoot left, I followed
them. Oh, stop it, journal. The constant questioning
of my actions becomes bothersome.

THE MOST AMAZING DISCOVERY EVER

So I followed him to where he lived in the woods.

It was awesomazable*!

He was building a bizarro machine. I asked him what
it was for. Instead of answering, he picked up a torch
and shone it into the trees, and...

It was like they were filled with stars!

I said it was magic. And he said yes! He said she
will come from the sky, and that she was like me.

Which is odd, because I'm not from the sky.

I'm from New Jersey.

NEW JERSEY

Facts from the desk of: **MAX**

Roxy Word: *awesomazable:

Max Fact: awesome + amazing +
incredible

20

I wanted to stay and see more magic, but it was late, and I had to get home. I asked if it was okay to come back tomorrow and visit Swiftfoot. The nice man mumbled something that sounded like "okay." On the way home I had a ROXA-REVELATION*. There was something about the lights in the sky and the magic that was familiar.

In my room, I went through my Tanaka books and found...
I knew it! The man in the woods talked about ceremonies, and magic, and lights in the sky...

⭐ HE IS A SHAMAN! ⭐

Facts from the desk of: **MAX**

Roxy Word: *Roxa-revelation:
Max Fact: Roxy + revelation

A SHAMAN

In Native American culture, a Shaman is kind of like a magic man. They communicate with the spirit world, and perform ceremonies.

A Shaman can...

1. Heal sick people.
2. Teach you about life.
3. Smite your enemies.
4. Make huge snowstorms so you can stay home from school.
5. Tell you what the spirit world wants you to learn.

Shamans often have people who help them perform ceremonies. They are called apprentices.

Hey! Roxa-revelation number two...

I COULD BE THIS SHAMAN'S APPRENTICE!

This morning, Mom, Jon, and me stopped in at MAYOR SAUL BLOOMBERG'S office to do some sesquisemteminal* stuff.

Mayor Saul is terrified of making a speech at the ceremony. Deputy Potts showed up with a crystal that is supposed to go in the sesquisemtunnel lighthouse. The crystal makes the beam of

light shine. But a LIGHTHOUSE? This town is a bajillion* miles from the ocean! (And a lighthouse is something that warns people away! Duh!) These Roxservations* made Deputy "Bull" Potts flustery and blustery. I don't think he likes people (especially young ones) questioning him.

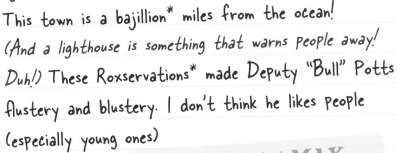

Facts from the desk of: MAX

Roxy Word: *bajillion:
Max Fact: a lot
Roxy Word: *Roxservations:
Max Fact: Roxy + observations
*sesqui + anything = sesquicentennial

23

DEPUTY POTTS

An analysis by Dr. Roxanne Hunter Froid*—famed sykologist*. Deputy Potts is not actually a mean man. But I think he is like one of those **puffy** fish. When they get scared or rattled, they **puff** themselves up to look bigger than they really are. And the other problem is that he's always eating these yucky candy bars called Lemon Boofoo that kind of make his breath smell bad. Minty gum might help.

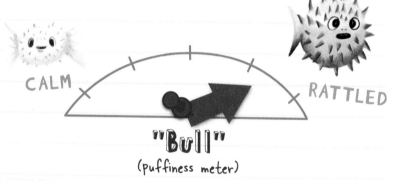

CALM   RATTLED

"Bull"
(puffiness meter)

Facts from the desk of: **MAX**

Roxy Word: *Froid:
Max Fact: Sigmund Freud: a famous psychologist

Roxy Word: *sykologist:
Max Fact: psychologist: someone who studies human behavior

Heartbreak Bulletin

Well.

That's it.

It's over.

Tragic, really.

What happened,

you ask, oh journal?

This is what I saw

on my way to day

camp. Max has left me for the *fiancé-filching* Jill.

What can I do but wish them happiness... NOT!

Max has obviously **LOST HIS MIND***!

Facts from the desk of: **MAX**

Max Fact: *I am just Jill's tutor.
That's all. Really.

Recovering from my horrible Maxa-revelation,
I continued with my investigation. I had to find out
what the "girl from the sky ceremony" was
if I was going to be a good apprentice. Once more
I entwisted* the help of my good ally and librarian,
Mr. Tibers. And guess what? He is friends with Lorne
Red Deer—an expert on all things Native American!
After some amplificated* convincing (shouting
"PLEEEEEEEASE" at the top of my lungs—
it always works) I got Lorne's phone number from
Mr. Tibers.

Facts from the desk of: **MAX**

Roxy Word: *entwisted:
Max Fact: enlisted

Roxy Word: *amplificated:
Max Fact: amplified: loud

I CALLED LORNE RED DEER.

He said that there was a ceremony called the
"Girl from the Northern Lights."

LIGHTS! Just like the lights in the Shaman's
trees! That must be it! Unfortunately our phone call
was rudely cut short by the warden Sauerkraut.
Just once I'd like to be on Ms. Slausen's good side...
If she even has one.

27

I AM AN OFFICIAL MASTER OF DECEPTION

After day camp (SNOOOOZEFEST), I went to see Swiftfoot. I brought him some cheese. I was going to bring him some animal crackers, but that seemed too much like CANNONBALLISM*.

However, just as I met him, I saw...

Seth and the neighborhood nitwits approaching!

They were looking for the Black Marsh Monster...

But I couldn't let them find the Shaman!

As his apprentice, I had to do something... FAST!

Facts from the desk of: **MAX**

Roxy Word: *cannonballism:*

Max Fact: cannibalism: animals eating their own species

Thinking rapidatiously*, I sent Swiftfoot away.
Then I ran to the kids and pretended I'd seen the
monster and that it tried to get evil, icy control
of my mind! I told them what the monster
wanted... (dramatic pause)

It wanted CHILDREN!

You should have seen them run!

HA! HA!

Suckers! I was considering a
career as a great actress, like
Audrey Heartburn*, when Mom called me to dinner.

WHEN DINNER GETS COLD

I notice that when a family hides things from one another, the dinner table gets quiet and cold. Mom got all quiet when I asked her about Jon. She's hiding something. I think they may be breaking up. Which is sad. I like Jon. Then Max let it slip that he had done HOME-WRECKER JILL'S homework for her! I have NEVER asked him to do my homework for me. Well, I have, but he just says no. What kind of maniputating* woman has he left me for?! Then it was my turn to go quiet when Mom asked me where the cheese was. I had to— I couldn't tell her about feeding it to my starving sidekick! The dinner may have been hot, but the conversation sure was cold. Brrr.

Facts from the desk of: **MAX**

Roxy Word: *maniputating:

Max Fact: manipulating: deviously controlling

This morning I have had it with day camp and Ms. Slausen! She got angry at me for feeding the fishes. How does she know they don't like bananas?! I am busting out of here first chance I get!
I am a Shaman's apprentice, and that is an important job! I have to help him prepare for the "Ceremony of the Girl from the Northern Lights"!

I have responsibilities!

I can't be chained here at the cut-and-paste academy, making macaroni art!

PUH-LEASE!

Oh boy. **I'M IN A PICKLE.**

So I dodged Slausen, and went to see the Shaman and Swiftfoot. The machine he is working on is amazing! (Although I still don't know what it does.) And he told me that our ceremony starts on **Saturday at 9:00 P.M.** sharp! That's the same day as the sesquicenteminal*. It was all great, until I saw something strange... There on the ground were the STOLEN FLAGS that Deputy Potts had talked about. And the Shaman had something else he shouldn't...

It was the CRYSTAL for the Serenity Falls Lighthouse! And then I got a sinky feeling in my stomach. He said he found it in a house in the

ground. But it doesn't belong to him. So I left.

And then on the way back into town, I saw...
Deputy Potts saying that the crystal had been
STOLEN!

Facts from the desk of: **MAX**

Roxy Word: *possum:

Max Fact: posse: a group of people summoned by the law

They were arranging a
search possum* to go find it!

I don't understand—the Shaman seems like a good
man—a little confusing, but a good man. I don't
think he would steal anything from anyone. But he
does have the crystal! And that sinky feeling in my
stomach has turned into an ache. I have to figure
out what to do.

WHEN LIFE GIVES YOU A DILEMMA, MAKE DILEMMONADE

a poem by Roxy Hunter

Sometimes you're in a confusing place,
And don't know what to do.

'Cause if you help **Person One**,
You will hurt Person Two.

And if you help Person Two,
You may hurt **Person One**.

Having to make this kind of choice,
Is really not much fun.

Roxy Word: *reepercushions

Max Fact: repercussions: the consequences

I found a good hiding spot to decide what to do next.

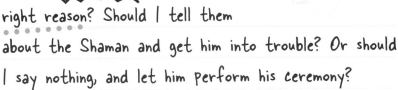

Should I do the right thing for the wrong reason, or the wrong thing for the right reason? Should I tell them about the Shaman and get him into trouble? Or should I say nothing, and let him perform his ceremony?

That's when Mr. Tibers found me. He said I should do the right thing despite the reepercushions*. Which was

what I was afraid he'd say. So it was time to face the music and talk to...

MOM

I went to the gazelbo* where she was decorating for the sesquicemential*.

I said I had to talk to her about something—and she thought it was about her and Jon. She told me that she had put their relationship on pause. "PAUSE?" What the heck is "PAUSE?" That's like saying you're breaking up with someone without actually saying you're breaking up with someone. Flibbersnibbits!

First me and Max—then Mom and Jon...
DOESN'T ANYBODY
STAY TOGETHER
ANYMORE?!
After all, we're not in Hollywood!

Facts from the desk of: MAX

Roxy Word: *gazelbo
Max Fact: gazebo

Just then, Mayor Saul came running up and said that the search possum had captured the crystal thief! They'd captured **THE SHAMAN!**
So I ran over to the sheriff's station.

The second I saw the Shaman, I knew in my HEART that he was innocent. I just knew it.
I tried to explain that to Mom and

everyone. I told them I was his apprentice, and we were preparing for a ceremony in the woods!

But when she found out that I knew the Shaman from before, Mom FLIPPED like an angry pancake.
Oh boy. I am in SO MUCH TROUBLE.

Princess Roxahana

Awaits the hangman's call.

Her DOOM lies just ahead,
Although she is not guilty AT ALL.

She holds herself up proudly,
Even though her heart sinks.

She NEVER, EVER was as bad,
As her mother thinks.

Facts from the desk of: **MAX**

Roxy Word: *verdiction

Max Fact: verdict: a judgment

Roxy Word: *payroll

Max Fact: parole: a conditional release of a prisoner

After the most silent car ride in history, I was sent to my room. After what felt like FOREVER, Max came in with the verdiction*.

GROUNDED FOR LIFE. NO CHANCE OF PAYROLL*.

Apparently being in the woods at night saving starving sidekicks and meeting Native American mystics is a fifteen on the bad scale.

And the scale only goes from one to ten.

But that wasn't the worst part…

The worst part was that Mom was disappointed in me. That makes me feel like a dark cloud has pushed my heart down into my shoes.

 I LOVE MY MOM.

And I try to make her proud.
But I just see things differently than her.
And she has a hard time with that because she lives in a Mom world—and I live in the real world.
Journal, it is so very hard raising a parent.
But the person I feel worstest* for is the Shaman.
Now he won't be able to meet the girl from the
Northern lights.

Facts from the desk of: **MAX**

Roxy Word: *worstest
Max Fact: the worst

Max believes in me! He said he thinks the Shaman is innocent! And I was right about the Max-nabbing Jill! She WAS up to something sinister! She was using him to do all of her homework! Now Max sees it, too! Take that, EVIL JILL!

Today is the day of the ceremony and the sesquisentimental. I am grounded.
So I can't leave the house.
So I need a sitter.
So guess who Mom got?

SAUERKRAUT SLAUSEN!

Flibbersnibbits!

And with me having to break the Shaman out of jail. Boy, they sure do make it tough on a nine-year-old. I need a plan.

HOW TO BAKE AN ESCAPE CAKE

Used for getting Shaman out of prison on the day of the "Girl from the Northern Lights" ceremony.

INGREDIENTS:

1 package of cake mix

1 carpenter's file from the toolbox
(perfect for filing down prison bars)

STEP 1: Follow directions for the cake mix.

STEP 2: Bake it.

STEP 3: When it has cooled,

INSERT FILE INTO CAKE.

STEP 4: Cover in icing.

STEP 5: Take to prison.

STEP 6: Free the innocent.

HOW I MADE A MEAL OUT OF SAUERKRAUT

They say beauty is on the inside.
But apparently most people want it on the
outside. Sauerkraut Slausen is no exception.
I told her that the icing for the Shaman's escape
cake was really a SECRET beauty cream that my
great-grandfather Horatio Hunter the Third
brought back from the So Yung Long province of
China (made up). I told her that my mom was
really forty-seven years old (made up). And that
she uses the cream to look as young as she does.

And she bought it!

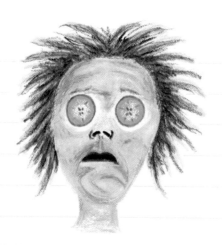

So I applied the icing to her face. I put some cucumber slices on her eyes. Then I played some sooooothing music and told her to relax—and not to move or say a word, otherwise the nutriments* would not be absorbed. And that's how you outwitilize* a Slausen, and get your **ESCAPE** cake to the imprisoned Shaman.

Facts from the desk of: **MAX**

Roxy Word: *nutriments
Max Fact: nutrients

Roxy Word: *outwitilize
Max Fact: outwit: to outsmart

WOWZEREE!

Oh, journal, you will not believe this. I don't even believe it my own self.

When I got to the jail to free the Shaman...

HIS CELL WAS EMPTY!

HE HAD ALREADY ESCAPED!

 HE IS MAGIC!

But instead of escaping, he started searching the station for his things.

He looked for them like they were treasure. And when he found his belongings, I could tell why they were more valuable than GOLD.

 Sarah

He showed me an old, battered photo. It was what he had been searching for. It was of a little girl. And, in that moment, I understood who the girl from the sky was.

It was his daughter. (Her name was Sarah.) And then I figured out something really, REALLY heartbreakering*—it explained the sadness in the poor Shaman's eyes...

His daughter had died. And I knew that his ceremony, the machine-thingy he built in the woods, was his way of trying to talk to her.

Facts from the desk of: **MAX**

Roxy Word: *heartbreakering
Max Fact: heartbreaking. And it really is.

46

MISSING PEOPLE

After my dad died, I used to attach little notes to balloons.

They said things like **"I LOVE YOU"**

and

"I MISS YOU,"

and sometimes they were just things about the day I'd had. I would let them go up into the sky, hoping that he would get them and read them.

 Time takes away the ache. But it doesn't take away the missing.

THE THINGS I DO WRONG TRYING TO DO SOMETHING RIGHT

I knew I had to help the Shaman.

I knew his sadness would not end until he could complete his ceremony and talk to his daughter.

I knew the crystal was an essentimental* part of his machine-thingy.

He <u>NEEDED</u> it. So I told him to go back to the camp and wait for me. I was going to get the crystal from the Serenity Falls Lighthouse.

BUT HOW?!

I had to come up with a super-cunning, extra-mastermindful* plan.

Facts from the desk of: MAX

Roxy Word: *essentimental
Max Fact: essential

Roxy Word: *mastermindful
Max Fact: a Roxyism

Getting the crystal was easier than I thought.
Backstage at the sesquimonterranial,
Mayor Saul was guarding the crystal.
He was very nervous about making his speech.

I made him more nervous.

I told him that television crews had showed
up and that he was going to do his speech in
front of MILLIONS of people (made up).
I have never truly seen a person turn
GREEN before. It was MOST disturbing.
He ran off, and I ~~stole~~ borrowed the crystal.

Of course when they unveiled the lighthouse, the entire town realized the crystal had been stolen—

AGAIN!

And then Deputy Potts told them that the Shaman had ESCAPED and attacked him.
(As if.)
Boy, did they get angry!

DEPUTY POTTS

They formed a search possum—but they didn't have to do much searching, because...

THEY KNEW WHERE WE WERE!

After running through the forest, I got to the campsite with the crystal. The Shaman placed it in the machine. Then he jumped on it, and started peddling like CRAZY!

BUT NOTHING WAS HAPPENING!

Then I saw flashlights and heard voices—the search Possum was about to find us! WE WERE RUNNING OUT OF TIME!

I was so scared that the Shaman wasn't going to be able to perform the ceremony!

At the lastest possiblest second, the Shaman hit a switch and... *I have never seen anything like it in my life. Everyone in the search possum froze. It was so beautiful.* And then...
She appeared in the light. It was the ghost of **Sarah**.

The funny thing is—I asked later and NO ONE ELSE SAW HER except the Shaman and me. I guess they don't have the benefit of being mysticalized* like us.

The Shaman talked to his daughter, and said what he wanted to say all these years.
It was "GOOD-BYE."

oh journal,
it would have wrung the tears from your pages.

BUT THAT'S NOT THE END OF THE STORY!

They took me and the Shaman and the crystal to the sheriff's station... **IN A POLICE CAR!**
Oh boy, were we in trouble.

At the station, I *(very nobly)* told them that it was **ME** that stole the crystal the second time.

But it didn't make a difference.

The Shaman was going to be sent to jail for stealing it the first time. We were DOOMED.

And it looked like I was going to be his apprentice on the chain gang!

But that's when dear, sweet, back-in-my-good-books **MAX** showed up

AND SAVED THE DAY!

HOW MAGNIFICENT MAX SOLVED THE MYSTERY AND REVEALED THE TRUE CRYSTAL THIEF!

This is what he did...

Max went to the campsite and saw some kind of mud there that is only found in the BLACK MARSH.

He bravely went to the Black Marsh and discovered a bomb shelter...

A HOUSE IN THE GROUND!

Just like the Shaman said!

Inside this bomb shelter *(puh–lease. Who would bomb Serenity Falls?)* he found the stolen flags and things. But, he also found...

A Lemon Boofoo wrapper!

And he knew that the only person in town who ever ate them was...

DEPUTY POTTS!

But why would Deputy Potts
steal the crystal, you ask?

Well, it was because he wanted to be the one
who found it...

SO HE WOULD LOOK LIKE A HERO!

But why? You ask—once again.

Because he got tired of people teasing him and
calling him "BULL" because of that one
Valentine's dance like a million years ago.
Everyone felt a little guilty about that.
I guess people don't realize how hurtful nicknames
and teasing can be.

Not even grown-ups.

So Deputy Potts was actually the Marsh Monster that Andy saw in the woods that night.

And the Shaman REALLY DID find the crystal in a house in the ground—the bomb shelter. **He was innocent!**

I was very proud of Max solving the mystery on his own—even without my help! Can you believe it? He makes a much better supersleuth than he does a French tutor.

Much, much better, indeed.

Facts from the desk of: **MAX**

Roxy Word: *planetararariums

Max Fact: planetariums

THE SECRET OF THE SHAMAN REVEALED!

Soon after, the Shaman's cousin showed up to take him home. It turns out that the Shaman had been a famous builder of lasers for planetararariums* and stuff all over the country. He flew his daughter out to see the opening of one of his biggest shows. But the plane didn't make it.

And she died.

I guess the sadness was so big inside him that some part of his mind went away with her.

Since then, he has wandered the country trying to build more laserlight things, thinking she will see the light and come back to him. His cousin told me he wasn't a real Shaman, and couldn't do real magic.

But then the Shaman told me...

> If something comes from the heart—
> then that is real.

I hope I helped to take a little of his sadness away.

If I were really a Shaman, this is the spell I would say for my Shaman:

SPIRITS OF

WATER, FIRE, EARTH, and AIR
Listen to me and hear my prayer
Heal this man's most broken heart
Let his loneliness now depart!

Maybe I'll try it, anyway. You never know...

THE ANTICLIMAX

So I went to the dance.

Mom and Jon made up (what was that all about?).

Jill asked Max to be her boyfriend when they were older... And he said NO.

HA. HA. HA.

(I wasn't worried for a second.)

But I still couldn't help feeling sad when I thought about my Shaman. I imagined what it felt like to grief* something so much that your life breaks along with your heart. So I left the dance. Looking up at the stars, I felt very alone. Just like the Shaman. And extremely just like Princess Roxahana, the near-orphan warrioress.

Facts from the desk of: **MAX**

Roxy Word: *grief

Max Fact: grieve

And that's when I saw what I saw.

AND I SAW IT! HONEST!

In the distance was a shimmery, glimmery sight.

It was Sarah! The ghost of the Shaman's daughter!

And with her was...

SWIFTFOOT!

She brought Swiftfoot to me knowing that he needed
a home, and I needed a sidekick. No. I needed a friend.

So there you have it—the Secret of the Shaman.

And the secret is... The love that comes from your
heart—that is the true magic!

Good night, dear journal.

the End